THE LAND OF GRAY WOLF

THE LAND OF GRAY WOLF

by Thomas Locker

A Puffin Pied Piper

Late one night during the Moon of Thawing Ice, a boy lay in his bearskin blanket and listened to a wolf howling. The boy, whose name was Running Deer, was too excited to sleep, for at dawn he was going to help set the forest on fire.

After several hours Running Deer got up and joined his parents and friends as they ate a small meal of ground corn and dried fish. The women and children then left the village to gather maple syrup while Running Deer, proud that he was finally old enough to go with the men, watched his father Gray Wolf put a glowing coal from the fire into a big clam shell. As the morning mist began to rise, Gray Wolf put the shell into a deerskin pouch that he carried, and the men entered the forest.

Several miles from the village Gray Wolf made a torch of birchbark and touched it to the hot coal. Swiftly he set piles of twigs and dry leaves on fire, and Running Deer stayed close to his father as the flames raced over the forest floor. The fire moved too quickly to harm the giant trees but it burned the dry grass and dead wood, and the thickets where animals could hide. The Indians worked hard to keep the fire under control, and as they walked back to the village at nightfall, Gray Wolf told his son, "The hunting grounds will soon be ready for spring."

A few days later Running Deer and some of his friends went to the burned forest where they saw that tender spring grasses had already begun to sprout from the ashes. Many animals came here to eat the grass, so there would be good hunting that spring. However, the Indians now had a new worry: White settlers were coming up the river.

One day several white men entered the village and offered the Indians guns, copper pots, and wool blankets in exchange for part of the hunting grounds. Some of the young men saw no harm in sharing the land with the settlers, whom they called Light Eyes.

But Gray Wolf disagreed. "The whites cut down many trees," he said. "There will be no more hunting and no place for us." So the Indians refused to let the settlers move onto the land.

With the coming of spring the forest animals grew fat. The Indians broke up into small hunting parties. Running Deer and Gray Wolf set up a camp near the waterfall and others went to snare migrating flocks of birds. When the leaves on the white oak were as big as the ears of a mouse, the women planted the garden.

That summer the hunting was good, but Running Deer and the other hunters only killed what was needed for food and clothing.

One afternoon while checking his bear traps, Running Deer looked across the river and saw smoke rising on land that a neighboring tribe had traded to the settlers. The smoke was coming from big fires they had set to clear away the trees for their farms.

Gray Wolf pointed at the smoke and said, "I am afraid that if the Light Eyes clear part of the land, they will one day want it all."

The settlers returned again and again to Running Deer's village, but Gray Wolf refused to trade with them. Sometimes settlers hunted on the Indian land anyway, and the Indians sent messengers to warn them to stop.

Then one afternoon while Running Deer was tracking a buck, he came upon a bright new clearing in the forest. Silently he crept closer and saw, to his horror, that many settlers with axes were cutting down the trees.

Running Deer raced back to the village to tell everyone that the settlers were destroying the hunting grounds. The Indians knew that they must protect the land or their own food supply would be destroyed. For several days they held council late into the night. One morning Running Deer watched Gray Wolf and the men as they chanted and danced, preparing for war. Then the men went into the forest to stop the settlers.

The Indians crept silently toward the whites who were cutting down the trees. When Gray Wolf gave a signal imitating the call of an owl, they attacked, surprising the settlers and driving them away.

That night the drums beat in a victory dance. The tribe was not happy for long, however. Settlers in greater numbers soon attacked the village, killing many—including Gray Wolf. They burned Running Deer's village to the ground.

Running Deer and his mother escaped into the forest. But the white men hunted them down, and at the first snow they were herded together with the other members of the tribe who were still alive. They were forced to go to a small, rough plot of land on a distant mountainside, which the whites called a reservation.

In his new home, when he lay awake at night listening, Running Deer no longer heard the howl of the wolf.

More and more white men arrived, taking the valley for their own, and stripping the hillsides of trees. They used the trees for firewood and to build houses and barns.

Running Deer grew to manhood on the reservation, surviving by trapping animals and trading their fur. He and his children watched the old hunting grounds fill up with farms surrounded by stone walls.

Year after year the farmers sowed their crops in the valley until the rocky soil was used up and could no longer produce healthy plants. They began to move away from the valley, going west or moving into distant cities. Sometimes their barns rotted and fell in, and small trees grew up in the abandoned pastures between the crumbling stone walls. Then forest animals began to return.

Today, the land of Gray Wolf is again covered by trees. Beavers dam the streams. Raccoons climb over the moss-covered stone walls, now nearly hidden in the undergrowth. More deer can be seen in the woods than ever before.

Some of Running Deer's people still live nearby on the mountainside. Perhaps one day they will hear the howl of a wolf echoing in the forest night.

For Aaron T. L.

My thanks to the staff of the American Indian Archaeological
Institute of Washington, Connecticut, for their invaluable assistance
in researching the ways that the first Americans lived.

PUFFIN PIED PIPER BOOKS
Published by the Penguin Group
Penguin Books USA Inc., 375 Hudson Street, New York, New York, 10014, U.S.A.
Penguin Books Ltd, 27 Wrights Lane, London W8 5TZ, England
Penguin Books Australia Ltd, Ringwood, Victoria, Australia
Penguin Books Canada Ltd, 10 Alcorn Avenue, Toronto, Ontario, Canada M4V 3B2
Penguin Books (N.Z.) Ltd, 182–190 Wairau Road, Auckland 10, New Zealand
Penguin Books Ltd, Registered Offices: Harmondsworth, Middlesex, England

Originally published in hardcover by Dial Books
A Division of Penguin Books USA Inc.

Library of Congress Catalog Card Number: 90-3915
Printed in the U.S.A.
First Puffin Pied Piper Printing 1996
ISBN 0-14-055741-5
A Pied Piper Book is a registered trademark of
Dial Books for Young Readers, a division of Penguin Books USA Inc.,
® ™ 1,163,686 and ® ™ 1,054,312.
1 2 3 4 5 6 7 8 9 10

The art for each picture consists of an oil painting
that is color-separated and reproduced in full color.

THE LAND OF GRAY WOLF
is also available in hardcover from Dial Books.